Dear Parents:

Congratulations! Your child is taking the first steps on an exciting journey. The destination? Independent reading!

STEP INTO READING® will help your child get there. The program offers five steps to reading success. Each step includes fun stories and colorful art or photographs. In addition to original fiction and books with favorite characters, there are Step into Reading Non-Fiction Readers, Phonics Readers and Boxed Sets, Sticker Readers, and Comic Readers—a complete literacy program with something to interest every child.

Learning to Read, Step by Step!

Ready to Read   Preschool–Kindergarten
• big type and easy words • rhyme and rhythm • picture clues
For children who know the alphabet and are eager to begin reading.

Reading with Help   Preschool–Grade 1
• basic vocabulary • short sentences • simple stories
For children who recognize familiar words and sound out new words with help.

Reading on Your Own   Grades 1–3
• engaging characters • easy-to-follow plots • popular topics
For children who are ready to read on their own.

Reading Paragraphs   Grades 2–3
• challenging vocabulary • short paragraphs • exciting stories
For newly independent readers who read simple sentences with confidence.

Ready for Chapters   Grades 2–4
• chapters • longer paragraphs • full-color art
For children who want to take the plunge into chapter books but still like colorful pictures.

STEP INTO READING® is designed to give every child a successful reading experience. The grade levels are only guides; children will progress through the steps at their own speed, developing confidence in their reading.

Remember, a lifetime love of reading starts with a single step!

DUNGEONS & DRAGONS®
HONOR AMONG THIEVES

Heroes Unite!

by Nicole Johnson

based on the screenplay by
Jonathan Goldstein & John Francis Daley

illustrated by Alan Batson and Grace Mills

Random House 🏠 New York

Welcome to the land of Faerûn! All sorts of people live across the land, in places like the tall Sword Mountains and the busy city of Neverwinter. Beneath Faerûn is the Underdark. And some unlucky people live in a snowy prison called Revel's End.

Edgin is a bard, which means he makes music and is friendly and brave. He used to be a hero, but now he is in Revel's End for stealing. Can he be a hero again?

Holga is also in Revel's End. She is
a barbarian, so she is a good, strong
fighter. She and Edgin both got caught
during a big heist. Their friends
escaped with the treasure!

Edgin and Holga want to be let
out of prison. They talk to a
council that will decide their
fate. Edgin is very convincing.
He is sure they will get out.

Edgin tells the council about
his daughter, Kira. He says
he only tried to steal the treasure
so he could take care of his family.

As Edgin tells his story, a new
council member enters the chamber.
The council member has wings!
Edgin and Holga get up and grab
him. They all jump out the window!

The council member uses his wings to land them safely on the ground. Edgin and Holga are free!

Edgin and Holga run away from the prison. After a long journey south, they see Neverwinter in the distance. They stop to make a plan.

They decide to go to the city and
get the treasure back—and Edgin's
daughter, Kira, too. Both are with their
old friend Forge.

Once they arrive in Neverwinter,
they quickly learn where Forge is.
He became Lord of Neverwinter!
He now lives in the city's castle.

Forge was a thief and a con man when Edgin and Holga met him. How did *he* become Lord of Neverwinter?

In the castle, Kira greets Edgin.
Edgin is happy to see his daughter,
but he learns that Forge lied to her.
He told Kira that Edgin only cared
about the treasure!
Kira walks away, upset.

Edgin and Holga meet with Forge.
Forge says that he became Lord of
Neverwinter to become a better
man in Kira's eyes. Then the
evil wizard Sofina walks into
the room!

Sofina is the reason Edgin and Holga got caught during their big heist. They are shocked that Forge is working with her.

Edgin and Holga try to leave,
but Sofina uses her powers to trap
them. Forge reveals that he will
never let Edgin have the treasure,
or Kira. They are his now.

Forge's guards lead Edgin and Holga out of the city. But Edgin will not leave without Kira. Edgin and Holga fight off the guards!

They need a new plan to save Kira and get their treasure. They know they cannot do it alone.

Edgin and Holga go to a nearby
playhouse. There, they see a sorcerer
performing a magic show.
The sorcerer is not very good.

The crowd is bored. They do not see the sorcerer using his magic to steal from them behind their backs.

The sorcerer is their friend Simon!
After Edgin and Holga were
arrested, Forge and Sofina tried
to hurt Simon. He has been hiding
from them ever since. He agrees to
help Edgin and Holga. And he
knows someone else who can help.

Simon leads Edgin and Holga
to a nearby forest. They look for
his friend Doric, but they only see
some guards arresting a wood elf.

Suddenly, an owlbear jumps out at
the guards! The guards run away,
and the owlbear transforms into
a person and frees the elf.
It is Doric!

Doric is a druid. She can shape-shift into all kinds of animals. She uses her skills to protect her friends. She agrees to help the group get Kira and the treasure back.

The group needs a plan. The vault
holding the treasure has magical
protection. They wonder how they
will get through. Simon knows a way.

Simon tells the group about a magical helmet. It disables nearby enchantments, like the spell guarding the vault. The group discovers that a paladin named Xenk had the helmet last.

Xenk is brave and kind. And he always tries to do what is right. Xenk agrees to help the group if they promise to share their treasure with the people of Neverwinter. They agree.

Xenk leads the group to where he
hid the helmet in the Underdark.
They get the helmet!

Each person brings something special to the team. Together, they are sure they can defeat Forge and Sofina, save Kira, and get the treasure to the people of Neverwinter!